SKELETON TOWER

THE ATLAS OF CURSED PLACES

SKELETON TOWER

Vanessa Acton

darbycreek

MINNEAPOLIS

Darby Creek
A division of Lerner Publishing Group, Inc.
241 First Avenue North
Minneapolis, MN 55401 USA

For reading levels and more information, look up this title at www.lernerbooks.com.

The images in the book are used with the permission of: © Jeremy Walker/The Image Bank/Getty Images (lighthouse); © iStockphoto.com/mustafahacalaki (skull); © iStockphoto.com/Igor Zhuravlov (storm); © iStockphoto.com/desifoto (graph paper); © iStockphoto.com/Trifonenko (blue flame); © iStockphoto.com/Anita Stizzoli (dark clouds).

Main body text set in Janson Text LT Std 12/17.5.
Typeface provided by Adobe Systems.

Library of Congress Cataloging-in-Publication Data

The Cataloging-in-Publication Data for *Skeleton Tower* is on file at the Library of Congress.
ISBN 978-1-5124-1322-9 (lib. bdg.)
ISBN 978-1-5124-1357-1 (pbk.)
ISBN 978-1-5124-1358-8 (EB pdf)

Manufactured in the United States of America
1 – SB – 7/15/16

For A.W., J.C., and C.C.—great sidekicks for jaunts to cursed places

CHAPTER 1

"I'll give you the short version: the girl dies at the end."

Morgan says this without looking up from her phone. She must be playing a downloaded game, because I know she's not getting any service out here. We've been on this twisting, narrow coastal "highway" for two hours, and it's a complete dead zone. Steep cliffs directly to our left. Super-dense trees on our right. Every so often I'll see an old-fashioned call box hiding in those trees, a few yards beyond the road. So in case the ancient family minivan breaks down, we can use one of those things to call for a tow. But as far as cell service goes, forget it. Which is why I'm bored enough to talk to my older sister about the series finale of *Reckoning*.

"Which one dies?" I ask. "The hot girl or the one who does magic?"

"I think they're both hot," says Morgan, eyes still glued to her screen. "Everyone on that show is hot. I would date anyone in the cast."

The minivan swerves, following a sharp bend in the road. I slide sideways in the backseat. My seatbelt digs into my collarbone. This has been happening every five seconds since we got on this road. My stomach is losing patience. "Mom, can you maybe ease up on the gas when you get to a curve like that?"

"Relax, Jason," my mom says from the driver's seat. My parents' motto. Just relax. Don't worry about taking a turn too fast and plunging off the side of a cliff, into the Pacific Ocean.

I glance out the window but can't see much because the fog is so thick. Try leaving your shower running for about a year, with the bathroom door closed and no fan. Then try driving through that kind of mist at sixty miles an hour. On a road shaped like a kindergartner's scribble. With basically three feet of clearance between that road and the edge of a cliff. And *then* try to relax.

"OK, but seriously, tell me what happens in the finale," I say to Morgan. "I don't care about spoilers. Who knows when I'll get to watch it myself?"

Finally Morgan looks up from her phone. "They'll have Internet at the lighthouse, won't they?" She aims the question at Mom and Dad.

"We didn't ask about that," says Mom. Of course they didn't. When was the last time Mom and Dad ever considered anything practical?

The road twists again. This time I hold on to the side door so that I won't lurch the other way and slam into Morgan.

"But who needs Internet when you're living the dream?" adds Dad.

This is one of Dad's favorite phrases. *Who needs—insert something people really need—when you're living the dream?* According to my parents, we're constantly "living the dream." Their dream. Or to be more accurate: their endlessly changing dreams, plural. By now I'm used to their habit of switching jobs and homes and school districts every two years. Six months ago, Dad was trying to make it big with online poker while Mom started her own food truck. Now we're on our way to their next random gig: tending a historic lighthouse in You've-Never-Heard-of-It, California.

"For those of us born in the twenty-first century, no dream is worth giving up the Internet," I mutter.

Dad twists around in the front passenger's seat to look at me. "Jason, I'm not liking this attitude."

"Maybe I'd have a better attitude if I hadn't been motion sick since noon." Or if my parents hadn't sold everything we owned except what could fit in this minivan. Again. Or if they hadn't decided to move in the middle of October, a solid two months into the school year. *Again.*

"Look, there's a sign for the lighthouse!" says Mom brightly.

I almost miss it, thanks to the fog. But I catch a glimpse as the car zooms past. Just your typical touristy sign: *Point Encanto Lighthouse, 2 miles.*

"We're almost there!" says Dad.

That's when the minivan veers off the road.

CHAPTER 2

Morgan screams. To be fair, I scream too. When you're inches away from plummeting into the ocean, you tend to freak out.

But I have to give Mom credit. Her reflexes are quick. She slams on the brakes, and the van lurches to an awkward stop with only one wheel hanging over the edge of the cliff.

"Okay, okay, nobody panic!" says Dad.

The van isn't technically moving anymore, but I can feel gravity tugging on it. Like when a seesaw is perfectly balanced for about half a second. And you know that it's about to tip to one side or the other. Except in this case, there's only one way our van might tip: forward, off the rock ledge.

"Can you put it in reverse, Meredith?" Dad asks Mom.

"No!" I shout. "Keep your foot on the brake, Mom! And put the parking brake on!"

Dad glances back at me. "Jason, I don't—"

"He just took driver's ed in August, Dad!" snaps Morgan. "I think the safety stuff is fresher in his mind than yours." This is a first: my older sister taking my side. If we weren't teetering on the edge of death, I would thank her.

"Okay, the parking brake is on," Mom says.

"We need to get out of the van," I say. "Like, *now*."

Morgan reaches for the handle of her side door—the side door facing away from the ocean. "Count of three?" she says, unlocking her seatbelt with her free hand.

"Just go," I say. "Trust me, I'll be right behind you."

Five seconds later we're all standing on the road, a few feet away from where the van is perched. "That was the weirdest thing," says Mom. But not like she's freaked out, the way a sane person would be. *Intrigued* might be the word. "It was like the steering wheel just turned all on its own. I had no control at all."

"Imagine losing control of a speeding vehicle on a road with sharp curves," I say dryly. "Especially when you get distracted reading signs. What are the chances?"

Morgan shoots me her classic *Just let it go* look. My parents don't even seem to hear me.

"Guess I'll go look for one of those call boxes and see if we can get a tow," says Dad. "Don't worry, guys, it'll be fine."

"As long as the van doesn't pitch into the sea while we're waiting for the tow," I point out.

"And as long as another car doesn't come hurtling around that curve in the road and slam into us while we're waiting here," Morgan adds.

"Well, look on the bright side," says Mom. "We're only, what, a mile away from the lighthouse?"

"I thought the sign said a couple miles,"

I say. The sign is only a few car lengths away, so I head over to check.

Yep: *Point Encanto Lighthouse, 2 miles*. But up close, I realize that isn't the only thing the sign says. Along the bottom, someone has scratched some graffiti into the metal. The tiny, jagged lettering is hard to read, but not impossible.

Beware the curse.

CHAPTER 3

"Tow truck's on the way," Dad reports a few minutes later. "But it might take a while."

"You think?" I say. "That's what happens when you take a job in the middle of nowhere."

"Okay, Jason, we really don't need the negativity right now," says Dad. The edge in his voice doesn't exactly sound like positive energy, but whatever.

"Here's an idea," says Mom, all cheery. "Why don't you and Morgan just head on up to the lighthouse?"

I gape at her. "On foot?"

"Sure. Just follow the road. It'll probably only take about half an hour. Dad and I will wait here with the van until the tow truck comes. You can tell Mr. Shen what happened so he knows why we're running a little late."

"Who?"

Morgan rolls her eyes at me. "The program director at the lighthouse. Mom and Dad's new boss. Sure, Mom, we'll do that."

Before I can protest, Morgan starts dragging me by the arm. She's been doing that since I was a baby and she was a one-year-old. I shrug her off but follow her up the road. I'm not looking forward to a two-mile walk along the edge of a cliff. Still, anything's better than dealing with parents who never admit anything's wrong.

***

I hoped I'd feel better when we got to the lighthouse. Safer. No such luck.

We've just reached the far side of the parking lot—which is empty except for one car. "There it is," says Morgan, like I can't see for myself. From where we're standing, we have a clear view. Or as clear as any view gets in porridge-level fog. There's a cute little whitish cottage. Next to it is a cylinder-shaped, glass-peaked structure—the lighthouse. And next to that is a narrow tower built of metal scaffolding. A revolving light is shining from the top of the metal tower, slicing through the fog in a slow arc.

Cozy-looking, sure. But this whole setup is perched on a ledge of rock that juts into the ocean—the "point" in Point Encanto. And it's about half a mile below us. Between us and our destination is a stairway with hundreds and hundreds of steps. On either side of those steps is a steep downward slope, ending way-too-many feet beneath us, where rock meets ocean.

"Holy mother of—"

Morgan cuts me off. "Relax, Jason. This is why railings were invented."

She starts her descent. I grab the guard rail and inch down the first few steps behind her. "Don't *you* start telling me to relax. Mom and Dad are bad enough. They'll be telling me to relax when the apocalypse hits."

A killer wind is rolling in off the ocean.

I wish I'd worn a heavier jacket. Or a life vest.

"I read online that there are three hundred steps," says Morgan over her shoulder. "You can count them if it makes you feel better."

It doesn't. Mostly because for some reason I can't stop thinking about that sign. *Beware the curse.*

To my left: steep drop, ocean. To my right: steep drop, ocean. Straight ahead: my older sister, practically skipping down the stairs.

To distract myself, I call to Morgan, "What else did you find out about this place online?"

"You mean you actually care for once?"

"Come on, Morgan, just talk to me."

Morgan always researches our family's moves in advance. She programs the numbers of local takeout places into her phone. She remembers the names of our parents' bosses and knows random details about their jobs. I don't bother with any of that. What's the point of cramming all that information into your head if it won't matter in another few months?

When I was little, I got super excited about my parents' work. But that's like being really invested in a new show that gets canceled after thirteen episodes. Not worth it.

"Well, it's one of the oldest lighthouses in the Bay Area." She has a fact for almost every one of the three hundred steps. When it was built. (1880.) The name of the nonprofit foundation that currently runs it. (Something Something Lighthouse Association.) How long it's been a museum. (About three years.)

"Did you read anything about the place being cursed?" I ask.

"What? No. Why?"

"No reason." I point to the metal tower's rotating light. "So that's the light Mom and Dad have to take care of?"

Morgan glances back to see where I'm pointing. Then she looks at the tower and shakes her head. "No, that's the skeleton tower. Its light is automated. It replaced the original lighthouse light in the sixties."

"Wait. If it's automated, what are Mom and Dad supposed to do?"

"Take care of the old light—the historic one. Do maintenance work. Give tours."

"Seriously? That's . . . so lame."

"I don't know why you sound surprised. You think everything they do is lame."

"Guilty as charged."

Finally we reach the bottom of the endless staircase. The front door of the cottage has a small sign on it: *Welcome to Point Encanto Lighthouse. Visiting hours: Wednesday – Sunday, 9 a.m. – 5 p.m.* Today's Sunday, and my phone says the time is 4:45. Since we only saw one car in the parking lot, I figure peak visiting time is over.

Morgan knocks. A short, balding guy with thick glasses answers the door. "Good afternoon! Are you here for a tour?"

"No, actually, our parents just got hired to work here," says Morgan. "Steve and Meredith Lewis. They're the new keepers. Are you Mr. Shen?"

The guy's face lights up. "Oh, yes, of course! Come on in."

We step inside. If a museum and a gift shop had a baby, it would look like this room. The walls are covered in info-panels.

Display cases are scattered around like an obstacle course. Off to one side there's a bookcase filled with touristy coffee table books, travel guides, a few atlases. Racks of postcards and key chains stand nearby. Then there's the counter, which has a cash register and a cutesy guest book. It's all vaguely a letdown. Mom and Dad could've sold postcards anywhere.

Morgan introduces us, then says, "Our parents should be here soon, but we had a little accident on the road."

Mr. Shen's smile crumbles. "Oh no," he murmurs. "Not already."

"What do you mean, not already?" I ask.

"Nothing," he says, too fast. "I'm just sorry their time here is off to such a rough start. This job is difficult enough as it is."

"How so?" I press. "Other than going up and down those insane stairs every day."

The question seems to make him weirdly uncomfortable. "Well, being forty-five minutes from the nearest town . . . balancing so many different duties . . ."

"I mean, they're not actually going to be lighthouse keepers," I point out. "Right? They'll be more like tour guides."

"Caretakers," says Mr. Shen. "And I do like to think of them as keepers, in the true sense of the word. They may not be operating the light, but they're guardians of this place's history."

"Okay. Sure. How hard can that be, though?"

Mr. Shen sighs and glances up at the ceiling. "Harder than you'd think, I'm afraid. Our last keepers couldn't handle the stress." He pastes on a fresh smile. "But your parents are made of tougher stuff. I could tell from our phone interview. Once I've trained them on the routine, I'm sure they'll be fine. Would you like to see your apartment while we wait for them to get here?"

Mr. Shen leads us up the back staircase, unlocks the door at the top, and shows us the cottage's private second floor. Three bedrooms, a bathroom, and a "kitchen nook," aka a closet-sized space with an oven and a fridge. At least it's furnished. There are even some dry goods on the tiny pantry shelf.

"Help yourselves to the food the previous keepers left behind," says Mr. Shen. He's clearly noticed me eyeing the box of frosted cereal.

"They must've left in a hurry," I say as I grab the box.

"They didn't give much notice, no," Mr. Shen admits. Quickly, he adds, "I can show you the light station itself if you'd like to see it."

"We don't want to impose," says Morgan. "If you have to be back downstairs in case visitors come . . ."

"Business has been pretty slow lately," says Mr. Shen. "And it's almost five. I'm not expecting anyone to show up. It would be my pleasure to give you a quick private tour."

He doesn't wait for us to respond. Morgan follows him. She loves this kind of stuff. I stuff a handful of cereal into my mouth and set the box back on the pantry shelf. That's when my hand brushes the piece of paper on the shelf.

I pull it down. It's an envelope. On the back someone has scribbled in pencil: *TO THE NEXT KEEPERS.*

Mr. Shen and Morgan are already halfway down the stairs. I don't call out to them. I just tear open the envelope. Inside there's a piece of paper with a short, handwritten note.

YOU'RE NOT SAFE HERE. THIS PLACE IS CURSED. CHECK THE ATLAS OF CURSED PLACES. *IT WILL EXPLAIN.*

GET OUT WHILE YOU CAN.

CHAPTER 4

It's fair to say I'm weirded out by this letter. But I don't know how to ask Mr. Shen about it. How do you bring up a curse in casual conversation? So I just stuff the letter in my jacket pocket and rush to catch up with him and Morgan.

I do my best to concentrate on Mr. Shen's tour. We head outside and enter the cylinder-shaped building—the light station. On the ground floor, Mr. Shen talks a lot about the clockworks. It's basically a giant crank full of interlocking gears. "When you turn this handle, it moves the counterweight over there." He points to a big hunk of heavy-looking metal, hanging from the ceiling by a rope. "That weight is connected to the lens at the top of the light station. So if you crank the weight up as high as it can go—about ninety turns of the counterweight—it rotates the lens."

"And why is that important?" I ask. Not to be rude. But not exactly as if I care, either.

"You'll see in a minute." We climb a set of metal spiral stairs. They bring us to the top room, which has glass windows all the way around. "This is the lantern station," says Mr. Shen. "And that's the lens." He points to the roundish mass of gleaming glass in the middle of the room. It looks like a giant Christmas tree ornament. Four curved panels, each with about a million ridges, almost like scales. "Inside this lens, there's a lamp," Mr. Shen goes on. To prove it, he opens up a little door set into one of the lens panels. Through the opening, I can see an ordinary-looking light bulb hooked up to some kind of pedestal. "It used to be an oil lamp. Eventually an electric bulb was installed. This one is only a thousand watts. But when it's lit and the lens rotates, the light reflects off the glass of the lens. The reflection makes the light seem brighter. It can be seen for more than twenty nautical miles."

"Do you ever actually use this light anymore?" Morgan asks.

"The Fourth of July, some years," says Mr. Shen. "But we keep it in working order all year round. You parents will be cleaning it regularly. That's our way of honoring what this light used to mean. It helped ships at sea steer clear of the rocks. It assured sailors far from home that they weren't forgotten."

I'm too edgy to listen to much more of this. It doesn't help that the room has a stuffy Old Place feel. Maybe I just need some fresh air. I notice a handrail running around the outside of the building, on the other side of the glass walls. "Is there, like, an observation deck out there?"

"The catwalk, yes." Mr. Shen checks his watch.

"Can we go out on it?" I ask.

"Hm? Oh, sure." Mr. Shen opens a glass-paneled door that I hadn't even spotted. "After you."

I step out onto the wrap-around deck. The view from the top of the light station is pretty sweet. It's starting to get dark, but the fog has faded a little. We're right on the edge of the point, so there's ocean on three sides of us. The waves crash against the cliffs like they have a personal beef with them. The beacon from the skeleton tower sweeps slowly over the water. It reminds me of a flashlight. One that's constantly looking for something, and coming up empty. Or maybe not. Maybe it can see things I'm missing.

The whole place feels far away from everything, and not in a bad way. In a *you're on your own but you can handle it* way.

We walk slowly along the platform, doing a loop of the lighthouse. The thought of the curse comes back to me. Maybe the vibe of the place is lying to me. Maybe we *can't* handle being on our own here. The previous keepers couldn't.

"Hey, look," says Morgan, pointing toward the steps. "There's Mom and Dad."

Sure enough, there they are. Two

distant, tiny figures making their way down the staircase.

"Excellent!" says Mr. Shen. He checks his watch again. "I'll go down and meet them."

"Mind if we stay up here another minute?" I ask him. Morgan shoots me a puzzled look that I ignore.

"No problem. Just don't break anything." He laughs awkwardly to let us know he's joking. We laugh back to be polite.

When he's gone, Morgan says, "Don't tell me you actually like it up here."

I kind of do. But that's not the point. I take the letter out of my pocket. "I just wanted to show you this before Mom and Dad get here."

She unfolds the paper and scowls down at it.

"I found it in the upstairs apartment," I add. "Doesn't it freak you out a little?"

"Maybe a little," she says matter-of-factly. She hands the paper back to me. "But, I mean, a curse?"

I don't say anything. She raises her

eyebrows at me. "Come on. I know the accident earlier was scary, but—"

"Sure," I say. "Forget it."

***

Mom and Dad are as cheery as ever. The car's fine. And Mr. Shen is super excited to meet his new keepers. Or maybe just super excited to go home. He says he'll be back tomorrow to run through their training. For tonight, he'll get out of our way and let us settle in. He locks up the old lighthouse, hands over our keys, and heads for the parking lot. Am I the only one who notices that he seems to leave in a hurry?

***

Here's how I don't want to spend my evening: carrying our luggage from the parking lot to the keeper's cottage. Down the three-hundred-step staircase. In thirty-mile-per-hour winds. In the dark.

But I don't usually get what I want.

Which is why I'm on step 117 with a wheelie suitcase at 6:30 at night. I'm seriously thinking about just hurling it down the remaining steps. But with the wind, that doesn't seem smart. I kind of want my clothes to stay out of the Pacific.

So I'm doing my best to wheel it down. That isn't really working. Dad, who went down ahead of me, has already reached the bottom and carried his load inside. Morgan's behind me with a duffel bag, gaining on me fast. At least this is our last load.

Suddenly the wind picks up by a factor of about a zillion. I pitch sideways and slam into the guard rail.

And then I flip *over* the guard rail.

CHAPTER 5

I let go of the suitcase and grab for the railing with both hands. I miss the top rung. And the other two metal rungs below that. And the chain link mesh in between.

Basically, I miss.

I hit the rocky slope and start to roll. Fast. I think I'm screaming, but mostly I'm fighting for a handhold. I claw at the rocks, the moss, the scrubby grass. Finally my grip snags on some jutting rock. I feel like I've been falling for ages, but actually I'm only about ten feet away from the steps. I can see the railing, lit up by the beacon from the skeleton tower. The blinding beam of light seems to be shining straight at me, without moving, even though I know it must be slowly rotating.

Morgan's shouting at me from the steps. "Jason! Hold on! Hold on, I'll call 9-1-1!"

"We're forty-five minutes from the nearest town!" I shriek.

"Okay, I'll get Dad and Mom, and we'll—"

"I can't . . . hold on . . . that long! Do something NOW!"

"Okay, stop panicking! You'll make it worse!"

"Make it worse?!"

"I mean, don't move! Hang on and don't shift position. Concentrate on keeping your grip." While she says this, she rips open my suitcase and pulls out a T-shirt. Then another. She starts knotting the shirts together.

The wind is battering me, but not like before. Just your average thirty-mile-an-hour wind now. The skeleton tower's light moves away. I can only see the bare outline of Morgan and the steps.

Seconds later, the light comes back around. Morgan has a seven-shirt chain now. She wraps the last shirt around her waist and ties it. She ties the other end around the top rung of the guard rail. "Okay, here I come." She climbs onto the first rung of the railing, then the second. Next she swings her leg over and climbs down the other side. Finally, she crouches down and starts edging down the slope, toward me. With her right hand, she still holds on to the railing. With the left hand she reaches for me. At a certain point, though, she can't get any closer without letting go of the rail.

So she does.

The skeleton tower light swings away again, but I can still see Morgan's general shape. She braces her right hand against the rocks and keeps inching forward, until her fingers brush mine.

I grab on, and she pulls. With my free hand I try to push up against the rock. My feet scramble for a hold. Between Morgan's pulling and my slither-climbing, I gain about three feet.

The light's back. Morgan and I are even with each other now. Together, we crawl the rest of the way back to the guard rail. Morgan braces me while I haul myself over the railing, and then she climbs back over too.

I sink down on the steps and try to breathe normally. I fail.

"That was *insane*," says Morgan. She's shaking so hard she can't untie her T-shirt rope from the rail. "What happened? How did you go over the railing like that?"

"It was a freak wind! It was, like, hurricane force."

"I didn't feel it."

"Well, I definitely did!"

"Okay, I believe you. I don't know how it's possible, but I believe you." She gives up on trying to undo the knot around her waist. She just sits down next to me on the steps. The T-shirt rope trails from her like some polyester snake.

The skeleton tower's beam pans away from us again. It slowly swivels out over the ocean. One V-shaped strip of water glows under its light, stretching almost to the horizon. But everything around it looks darker, more shadowy than it actually is.

Something makes me reach into my jacket pocket. Empty. The letter from the previous keepers must've blown out.

"Morgan," I say. "What do you think the *Atlas of Cursed Places* is?"

She sighs. "I have no idea."

I keep watching the light from the skeleton tower. It's coming back around toward us again. Closer, closer.

"I think we should find out," I say.

CHAPTER 6

There are certain things you don't bother trying to explain to your parents. Especially parents who think bad things don't exist. Just bad attitudes.

A curse? Turn that frown upside down, Mister.

When Morgan and I straggle up the stairs with our luggage, we find Dad humming show tunes in the kitchen. "There you are," he chimes. "You two took your time. Mom's already in the shower, *annnnnd* dinner is served."

He gestures dramatically at the kitchen counter. Six open cans of beans await us.

You can see why the food truck idea didn't pan out.

"Dad, did Mr. Shen give you the Internet password?" asks Morgan. "We have to look something up."

Before Dad can answer, Mom's scream almost shatters my eardrum.

"Meredith?" calls Dad. "You okay?"

The first answer is the sound of the bathroom door rattling. Not opening, just rattling, like someone was jiggling the doorknob. The second answer is Mom saying, "Ummm . . ."

Morgan sprints over to the bathroom door. "Mom? What's wrong?"

"Well, the water's scalding hot and I can't seem to get it to turn off. And the tub is full of cockroaches."

"What!?" I burst out. I join Morgan in front of the bathroom door. I can hear the shower running inside. It sounds like it's on at full blast.

"And," Mom adds, "I can't get the door open."

Morgan grabs the handle and shoves. Then pulls. Then shoves again. No dice.

"Mom, stand back," I say. "We'll kick it in."

"Whoa, Jason," says Dad. "It's probably just swelled shut. That can happen with a wooden door if there's a lot of water vapor . . ."

"Well, if the shower won't turn off, there'll be even more water vapor pretty soon," I snap.

"Mom, how many cockroaches are there?" asks Morgan.

"Uh—well—none now."

"Wait, what?"

"They've—disappeared. Back down the drain. They were swarming all over the tub for a minute, but—now they're gone."

Morgan looks at me. I say, "Mom, I'm breaking down this door in two seconds."

Morgan steps back.

I'm not sure how I'm going to pull this off. I've never taken kung fu or anything. But I've hit my limit for weird dangers and dangerous weirdness. Slamming my body into a door seems like a reasonable response.

But suddenly the sound of running water stops.

"Huh," says Mom. "Looks like it's off now." She's trying to sound casual, but her voice is pretty shaky.

"You mean it turned off by itself?" I ask.

"Yeah. I guess."

Morgan clears her throat. "Okay . . . try the door again then."

"The wood still might be—" Dad starts.

The door opens.

Mom peers out. With one hand, she grips the doorknob. With the other she's clutching the towel around her waist. She actually looks more spooked now than she did earlier today, when our car almost went off a cliff. Go figure.

"I—um—I think I'll wait until tomorrow morning to wash my hair," she says.

"Can we also call pest control in the morning?" asks Morgan. "Because, you know, cockroaches."

"I think I just imagined them," says Mom.

"*Imagined* them?" I echo. "Mom. When was

the last time you saw something that wasn't really there? College?"

She chuckles awkwardly. "It's been a long day. I think we're all just tired and tense. And with a brand new place to get used to . . ." She shook her head like she was impatient with herself. "I'll just grab some clothes from my suitcase and get dressed. Then we'll eat and go to bed. We can get a fresh start in the morning."

She scurries out of the bathroom as Dad says, "Sounds like a plan!"

Accurate. My parents always have a plan. Just not usually a very good plan.

While Mom ducks into one of the bedrooms, Morgan turns to dad. "So: the Internet password?"

Mom accidentally left the bathroom light on. I step into the bathroom to turn it off.

The condensation on the mirror catches my eye. Because some of it has been wiped away. In the shapes of letters.

BEWARE LAURA LEE

CHAPTER 7

Forty minutes later, Mom and Dad are asleep. Morgan and I are very much awake, sitting on the floor of her new bedroom. She has her laptop open and is typing at eighty miles an hour. I'm trying not to throw up. The beans didn't agree with my stomach. Neither does the curse, probably.

"Look up 'Laura Lee' and see what you get," I say.

Morgan rolls her eyes. "I know what I'll get. A bunch of people's selfies. It's just an ordinary, common name."

"An ordinary, common name that showed up on our bathroom mirror."

"According to you, anyway."

"What's that supposed to mean?"

She glances toward me, then away. "Nothing. Just, you're the only one who saw it."

True. By the time I grabbed Morgan and dragged her into the bathroom, the writing on the mirror had disappeared. There was just a smudge of clear glass, as if the condensation had naturally dried. But I know what Morgan really means.

"You think I'm making this up?"

"No. It's just that—you always hate moving. You always find reasons not to like wherever we end up."

"That's not what this is," I say. "Look, it would be one thing if I was the only one seeing stuff, or feeling stuff. But Mom and the cockroaches? Plus the accident on the way here. *Plus* the note from the previous keepers."

"Fine! So this lighthouse is haunted."

"Well, cursed."

"Whatever." She scowls at her laptop screen. "I'm not getting any useful hits for *'Atlas of Cursed Places.'* I don't think it's real."

"Then try 'Point Encanto Lighthouse, cursed.'"

"Thanks, Sherlock. I already tried that while you were washing the dinner spoons. Nothing."

"Well, Mr. Shen knows something. Remember what he said when we got here? It seemed like he *expected* things to go wrong for us. Maybe we can get him to tell us more tomorrow."

"Maybe." Morgan looks doubtful.

I think about all the random stuff Mr. Shen told us during our tour. Too bad none of it will help us deal with a curse.

Something else occurs to me, though. "Let's go downstairs."

Morgan looks like she might laugh. "You want to check out the museum? *You?*"

I don't tell her what I have in mind. Just in case I'm totally off base.

Morgan follows me out of her room.

We creep to the front door of the upstairs apartment, which my parents didn't bother to lock. Probably because they weren't expecting Laura Lee, or anyone else, to get past the locked main door of the cottage.

I open the apartment door as quietly as I can and step onto the landing of the staircase. Morgan closes the door behind us. "There's a light switch right at the top of the stairs," she whispers.

I find it. And it doesn't work. I flick it a few times, then give up.

"Let's just use our phone lights." I take my phone out of my jeans pocket and activate the flashlight feature. I'm not saying I like the idea of going down those stairs in the mostly-still dark. Not after my experience on the outdoor steps. But at least I only have thirteen steps to deal with this time, instead of three hundred.

And I hold on pretty tightly to the banister.

We reach the first floor without tripping, falling, or seeing cockroaches. So far so good.

The visitors' center looks way creepier in pitch blackness. Most places do, I guess.

The light from the skeleton tower shines in through the little window in the front door. That light reflects off the glass display cases and the shiny surfaces of the postcards. Every dim shape in the room reminds me of a wild animal in a nature show: crouched, watching us, waiting to move.

Morgan feels around for another light switch. I head straight for the bookcase near the counter. I pan my phone light over the titles of the books, starting with the top shelf. This feels like a long shot, but I know I spotted a couple of atlases in this mix.

"Ugh, I give up," says Morgan. "We'll just have to keep using our phones." She starts examining the wall displays. A minute or so later she says, "This place was closed down for longer than I realized. Right after the skeleton tower was built, the original light station and cottage were abandoned. They were empty until just a few years ago. That's when the foundation started fixing things up."

"You're not seeing anything about anyone named Laura Lee?"

"I'm not seeing any names at all. This is all vague information about lighthouse keeping in general. What are you doing?"

Currently I'm squinting to read the title of a slim volume. It turns out to be *Top Ten Lighthouses of the Western World*. Next to that is *Lighthouses through Infographics*. "I'll tell you when I'm done. Carry on, Captain."

She snorts quietly. I haven't called her that in a long time. It really used to annoy her. Of course, when she was fourteen and I was thirteen, everything about me annoyed her, and vice versa. That hasn't changed. Much.

On the bottom shelf I find a bulky book with no title printed along the spine. I pull it out to get a look at the front cover.

I don't know what I was expecting. Some dusty old volume, I guess. But this book looks brand new. It has a glossy cover that blends in with all the other souvenir-type offerings. A generic color photo of the Earth seen from space. A businesslike font for the title.

But that title is definitely not tourist-friendly.

"Morgan," I say, "it's here."

"What's here?" she says, still shining her phone along the walls.

I hold up the book. "The *Atlas of Cursed Places*."

CHAPTER 8

Without warning, the lights flicker on. Then off again. Then on. Then off.

Then they stay off. But that doesn't stop Morgan and me from sprinting up the stairs. I clutch the book in one hand and my phone in the other. When we get to the landing, Morgan practically body-slams the apartment door.

It doesn't open.

"You've got to be *kidding* me," she growls. "This place is definitely haunted."

"Cursed."

"What's the difference?!"

"I don't know, but I assume there is one!"

The logical next step would be to pound on the door. Mom or Dad would wake up and let us in.

Of course, they'd also ask questions. Questions we don't yet have answers for.

"It might just unlock on its own eventually," Morgan whispers. "Like the bathroom door did for Mom."

"Yeah," I agree. "But in the meantime what do we do?"

She shrugs. "Wait at the top of the steps?"

Something about that idea doesn't appeal to me. Probably the *steps* part. I'm still a little squeamish after almost getting blown out to sea.

"Or . . ." I start.

She cuts me off. "I'm not going back downstairs. That light show almost gave me a seizure."

I raise my eyebrows at her. Even though she probably can't see them in the dark. "Morgan, are you actually scared?"

"Well, I'm *kind of* stressed out at this point, yeah."

"Stressed out or scared?"

"Stop splitting hairs! You're so immature."

I shouldn't smile, but I do. She probably can't see that either. For the first time in, well, our lives, I feel like we're on even footing. Equally scared. Equally clueless.

"Okay, well, if you're too *stressed out* to be in the visitors' center, we could go outside."

There isn't actually a clap of thunder at that moment. But we both pause, listening for one.

***

It's freezing outside. Welcome to October in the Bay Area. It's also incredibly dark. Like wearing a blindfold. Except for the rotating light of the skeleton tower. Tonight that beacon reminds me of an action movie hero, surrounded by enemies. Spinning around in a circle, pointing a weapon at all the bad guys. Not ready to accept being cornered.

Morgan crosses her arms to block the wind. "Well, I feel a whole lot safer out here."

"Hey, beggars can't be choosers."

"Fair enough. Where do you want to sit

and read this thing?"

The beacon swoops overhead, and I catch sight of something. At this point, what I see doesn't surprise me. And it only mildly creeps me out. "How about the old lighthouse?"

"Isn't that locked up for the night?"

"It should be. But the door's wide open."

Morgan sucks in a breath through clenched teeth. "Figures."

***

We stand in the doorway of the lighthouse. From what we can see by the lights from our phones, the first-floor service room is empty. No burglars. Or cockroaches.

"You sure it's a good idea to come in here?" hisses Morgan.

"Nope. But you're not cool with the visitors' center and I'm not cool with the stairs. So this is what's left."

Morgan shoots a nervous glance at the door. "Should we leave this open?"

"It doesn't seem to matter," I say. "The curse does whatever it wants."

"You mean the *ghost* does whatever it wants. Curses can't *want* anything."

"Like you're an expert. Here, let's find out what the atlas has to say about this."

"Actually, let's go up to the lantern station," says Morgan. "That way we'll have the light from the skeleton tower, shining through the glass."

I take a deep breath. "Okay, Captain. After you."

She leads the way up the spiral steps to the glass-walled room at the top. She was right about there being more light up here. I'm not sure if that makes the place less creepy or more so.

We sit down on the wood floor near the giant lens. I set the book on the floor between us. Morgan flips it open. "I guess we should check the index," she says. I hold my phone light over the pages while she thumbs through them. "Okay—California . . ."

She flips to the right page. It looks like an ordinary map of the state. Until you see the tiny skull icons stamped at various spots. "Are those the cursed places?" I ask.

"Looks like it." Morgan traces her finger along the west coast. "Oh man, Jason. Here it is. Point Encanto Lighthouse. And it says 'see page 31 . . .'"

She flips forward a few pages. And there's a lovely brochure-type photo of our new home. In daylight, on a day with no fog, it looks innocent. Cute. Almost boring.

I lean closer and start reading the text for the entry.

Point Encanto Lighthouse has carried a curse since the year 1887. This curse targets the light's keepers and their families. It is most active between sunset and midnight. Shortly before the curse was first reported, Seth Blake (1830–1888), the lighthouse's first keeper, allowed the light to go out during a storm. The date was October 25, 1887. Without the light to guide them, the merchant ship Laura Lee *steered too close to Point Encanto's rocks. The ship was wrecked, and most of the crew drowned. The doomed sailors of the* Laura Lee *are believed to have laid a curse on the lighthouse's keepers.*

"*Laura Lee*," I whisper to Morgan. "Not a person. A ship."

Morgan nods. "We're being haunted by a ship," she murmurs.

"Cursed by a ship."

"What*ever*."

Due to his lapse, Blake was dismissed from his position. He then suffered a nervous breakdown. The next keeper, Alva Waggener (1845–?), disappeared without a trace in 1889. Later keepers were often struck by severe health problems. Others were injured in freak accidents. In 1904, a fire nearly destroyed the keeper's cottage. In 1913, the roof of the cottage collapsed during a storm . . .

"Morgan," I mutter. "I know I've said this before. But this might actually be the worst move Mom and Dad have ever made."

CHAPTER 9

We skim through the rest of the lighthouse's history. "Seems like the curse calmed down after the skeleton tower was built," Morgan notes. "No more fires or whatnot."

"Well, there weren't any keepers after that," I say. "And the curse was targeting the keepers. So it makes sense that all the weirdness would've stopped. At least until a few years ago, when the old lighthouse reopened."

"Didn't you say earlier that Mom and Dad aren't *real* keepers, though?"

"I'm not sure the curse cares."

Based on what's happened today, Morgan can't argue with that.

We read the last paragraph of the entry.

Emma Blake Shields (1871–1967), the daughter of keeper Seth Blake, mentioned the curse in several family letters. Shields herself worked as a lighthouse keeper. She tended the Martine Bay Lighthouse for more than fifty years and had a spotless record. She is thought to have kept a diary during her family's time at Point Encanto Lighthouse. This diary, which has never been located, may contain further references to the curse.

Morgan's been running her finger along the page as she reads. When she reaches the final period, her finger flutters, like it's not sure what to do now.

"Wait, that's it? It doesn't tell us how to break the curse?"

"Apparently not," I say.

"But we have to figure out how to break it," says Morgan.

"Or we could just leave," I suggest. "I mean—convince Mom and Dad to leave."

She glares at me. "You're the one who's

always complaining that we never stay in one place."

"Yeah, well, most places we've lived haven't been cursed!"

Morgan makes a disgusted noise in her throat. "That's no excuse." She slams the atlas shut.

"How is that not an excuse? We could get seriously hurt if we stay here, Morgan!"

"I get that, Jason. But Mom and Dad aren't just going to pack up and leave. We haven't even been here twenty-four hours. And you know they wouldn't buy into the supernatural stuff. Besides, even if we could get them to quit, we'd be leaving this mess for the next keepers to deal with. That's not exactly fair, is it?"

Morgan's a fan of fairness. And of disagreeing with me.

"Our best bet is to try to break the curse," she insists.

"Before it breaks us," I say darkly.

"Exactly."

"And how do we do that?"

She stands up and crosses her arms, like

she's cold again. "I don't know. I don't even know if we can get back into our rooms."

I check the time on my phone. "The atlas said the curse is most active between sunset and midnight, right?"

"Right. So?"

"So, it's 12:02. Let's see if our apartment door is unlocked again."

***

We make our way back down the winding stairs of the lighthouse. Each metal step clangs under our feet. The acoustics in this lighthouse are pretty good. We're creating a massive echo.

The front door is still open, letting in a brisk sea wind. We sprint outside. Behind us, I hear a creak of hinges, and then a bang. The lighthouse door just shut itself.

***

We have no trouble getting back into the cottage. Ditto with the second-floor apartment. We agree to get some sleep and come up with a plan in the morning.

In my new bedroom, I step over my suitcases and set the atlas on the dresser.

The words of the previous keepers' letter come back to me.

Get out while you can.

For the first time, I realize I don't know for sure who wrote that letter. It *could've* been the previous keepers. Or . . .

It could've been whatever wrote *Beware Laura Lee* on our bathroom mirror.

It could've been the dead sailors, giving us fair warning.

***

I wake up to the sound of a voice downstairs.

I jolt upright, my heart break-dancing in my chest.

"Good morning, keepers! Ready for training?" The voice belongs to Mr. Shen.

I exhale slowly. The ghost-sailors of the *Laura Lee* haven't invaded the cottage. Or if they have, they're keeping quiet.

"Come on up, boss!" Dad hollers down the stairs.

Mom knocks on my door. "Rise and shine, kids! The shower's working fine now!" From her tone, you'd think last night's incident was just an ordinary plumbing glitch. "If you hurry you can job-shadow us!"

"Greaaaaat," I moan. "Living the dream."

Job-shadowing my parents is pretty much the last thing I want to do. But maybe Mr. Shen knows something about the curse. Maybe if Morgan and I tag along for Keeper Orientation, we'll get some useful information out of him.

I reach for my phone on the dresser. My hand grazes the *Atlas of Cursed Places*.

Which is lying open.

I sit up and stare at it. It was closed when I set it on the dresser last night. But now it's open to the Point Encanto entry.

And the bottom corner of the right-hand page is folded over. A triangle of creased paper now covers the final word of the entry. Which is, of course, *curse*.

I reread the entry's last sentence. And suddenly I know what we have to do.

Mom herds me into the bathroom before I can tell Morgan about my idea. I shower and dress in record time. And not just because I'm half-expecting to see cockroaches in the tub.

As soon as I get out of the bathroom, Dad shoves a doughnut at me. "Mr. Shen brought us breakfast! And sandwiches for lunch, too. And he says you and Morgan can tag along for our training. Sweet deal, right?"

He claps a hand on my shoulder and steers me toward the door. "Come on, we're about to start."

Mom, Morgan, and Mr. Shen are all waiting by the stairs, doughnuts in hand. "Morning, Jason," says Mr. Shen brightly. Too brightly. The smile, the doughnuts—the man is trying too hard. "Feel free to eat as we go. As long as you don't leave crumbs on any historic equipment." That nervous laugh again. Too nervous.

We all traipse downstairs. While Mr. Shen explains the ins and outs of the cash register to Mom and Dad, I whisper in Morgan's ear.

"Emma Blake."

"What?"

"*Shh*. Emma Blake. The first keeper's daughter. The atlas said she kept a diary. Maybe it's still here. Maybe we can find it. It might tell us how to break the curse."

Morgan chews thoughtfully on her doughnut. "Yeah. I mean, obviously. But how are we supposed to find it? The atlas didn't leave any clues, did it?"

I glance toward the info session we're ignoring. "Shen might know. He knows more than he's letting on. Remember yesterday? He made sure to leave before sunset."

She gives me a fraction of a nod. "Good point. Let's see if we can squeeze anything out of him."

We spend the rest of the morning trailing after Mr. Shen and our parents. I have to admit, some of the training is actually interesting. Like learning exactly how the original light works. How to turn on the electric bulb that sits nestled inside the giant lens. How to crank the gears and pull the weight that moves the lens. But the window-cleaning routine? The *floor*-cleaning routine? Not as cool.

Finally we take a break for lunch. As we all climb down the lighthouse steps, I place myself behind my parents and in front of Mr. Shen. Morgan brings up the rear. Halfway down the stairs, I stop. Mom and Dad are chatting excitedly about their keeper duties, so they don't notice. "Everything okay, Jason?" asks Mr. Shen, a few steps above me. "Just a second," I say, bending down. "Shoelace came untied."

I fiddle with my perfectly tied lace until Mom and Dad reach the bottom of the steps. I can't see them anymore because of the stairway's curve. But I hear them go outside, still talking. Meanwhile, Morgan takes her chance.

"Mr. Shen, do you know anything about the Blake family?" she asks.

There's a long, heavy pause. "Oh, the first keeper? Not much. We don't have many records from the early years."

I straighten up and turn to look at him. Definitely too nervous.

"It seems like Seth Blake was here longer than

any other keeper," pressed Morgan. "From 1880 to 1887. The others only lasted a couple of years."

"Yes, well, it was a demanding job."

"You've mentioned that," I said.

He glances at me for just a second. Then his eyes slide away. We were wise to block him in. The stairs are too narrow for him to squeeze past me. And I can tell he's wishing that wasn't the case.

"But lots of people spent decades doing it," Morgan plows on. "In fact, didn't Seth Blake's daughter become a lighthouse keeper? And didn't she have that job for ages?"

"I'm not sure." He glances at me again. "All set, Jason?"

"We're actually really interested in Blake's daughter," I say. "Emma, right? Have you ever heard anything about a diary that Emma Blake might have kept?"

That completely throws him off. "I—can't say I have. Sorry. Um, I don't know about you but I'm pretty hungry. Ready to go eat?"

Not quite. "Mr. Shen, do you think the lighthouse is cursed?"

Morgan grimaces. She was probably hoping I'd play it smoother. But I'm more interested in Mr. Shen's reaction.

Behind his glasses, his eyes get huge. "Who told you it's cursed?"

I cross my arms, hoping I look tough. "That's not an answer. In fact, you haven't answered any of our questions."

"We just want to know what we're dealing with here," adds Morgan. "Anything you can tell us would be helpful."

"I, uh, I'm glad to see you two have strong imaginations. That's a great thing in young people—"

"Fine," I say, turning around. "Don't tell us. Just don't be surprised when we leave like the other keepers did."

I start down the stairs again. Mr. Shen actually grabs my arm to stop me. "Hold on—I—that's not what—I mean it would be such a shame if—"

"If you had to go through the hiring process all over again? Yeah. I bet it would be. So what can you tell us?"

He lets go of my arm. In a low, unsteady voice, he says, "All I know is this. Emma Blake is part of the reason we have the skeleton tower. She pressured the Coast Guard for years. Pushed them to give Point Encanto an automated light. It was finally installed in 1967. And there haven't been any deaths or injuries here since then. If there was ever a curse, I think the skeleton tower laid it to rest."

"What about the previous keepers?" I ask. "The people who worked here before Mom and Dad? Something scared them off."

Shen mumbles something.

"What was that?" says Morgan.

"Just little things," he says more clearly. "Nothing truly dangerous. They had no reason to be alarmed. And neither do you."

I look over Shen's shoulder, at Morgan. She doesn't seem any more convinced than I am.

But now Mom's voice ripples into the lighthouse. "Hey, what's the holdup?"

"Just chatting," I say, clattering down the steps. "No reason to be alarmed."

CHAPTER 10

Mr. Shen wraps up the training session and heads home by sunset. Of course. "We'll take care of locking up," Dad says to us. "You two can get started on dinner!" He says this with an exclamation point, like it's a huge adventure.

Or we can work on breaking a curse, I think. I keep remembering how the atlas opened overnight. That didn't seem like the work of the curse. It was too helpful.

Morgan and I start up the back stairs of the cottage.

"We need to drive into town tomorrow and get some real groceries," Morgan says—right before we smell the smoke.

We both swear and sprint up the rest of the stairs. The good news: the apartment door opens for us.

The bad news: all four burners of the kitchen stove are lit.

"Doesn't this place have a smoke detector?" I shout. But I have a feeling the curse knows how to disable smoke detectors.

We rush to the stove and each turn off two burners.

They stay lit.

"I'll get the fire extinguisher," says Morgan.

She dashes off. I stay frozen, staring at the flames. Until I hear a *bang* downstairs. A few seconds later, Mom yells up, "Guys, I need the first aid kit!"

I couldn't remember the last time my mom sounded truly panicked. I forget about the stove. I run toward the bathroom, where the first aid kit is. "Mom? What happened?"

"Hurry up, Jason!"

Seconds later I'm downstairs in the visitors' center, carrying the plastic box. Dad is half-lying, half-sitting on the floor near the door.

Mom is crouching next to him. She's pressing one hand to the side of his head.

"Dad, are you okay?"

"He needs some antiseptic cream and a bandage," says Mom shortly.

I open the kit and hand her the cream. "What kind of bandage? Sheer, tough strip . . . ?"

"Actual gauze, Jason, not a little plastic one." She snatches the kit from me. When she moves her hand away from Dad's head, I see the gash.

Yeah. A tough strip isn't going to cover it.

"What happened?"

"Hit my head on the door," says Dad. He sounds like he's trying to laugh but can't quite pull it off. "Or more like the door slammed itself on my head."

Mom starts unwinding a roll of gauze. Her hands are shaking. I've never seen her this agitated.

"Do we need to take you to a hospital?" I ask. "You could have a concussion . . ."

"No, no, it's no big deal," says Dad.

Which is when all the information panels fall off the wall. They slam to the ground in perfect sync. In the tiny visitors' center, the noise sounds like gunfire.

Mom and Dad both flinch. Okay, I do too.

And then all the display cases shatter.

Bits of glass fly everywhere. I duck, but that's pointless. I still get hit with a spray of shards. Mom screams. Another first.

And Morgan calls from upstairs, "The fire extinguisher isn't working either! And it's spreading, Jason! The fire is spreading!"

CHAPTER 11

At this point, I call 9-1-1. So what if it'll take the emergency crews forty-five minutes to get out here? I see zero other options. "Yeah, we've got a fire and some injuries at the Point Encanto Lighthouse . . ."

As I end the call, Morgan tramps downstairs. "It's out," she says flatly. "Just went out by itself. It . . ." she trails off as soon as she gets a good look around. "Holy . . ."

"Yeah," I say. The visitors' center looks like a war zone. "Better not come all the way down the stairs. There's glass everywhere."

"You're all cut up," she says.

"Thanks, I hadn't noticed."

Actually, I'm only bleeding in a couple places. Mom and Dad don't look too bad either, aside from Dad's head wound. But their expressions—I almost don't recognize them.

For the first time that I can remember, they look scared. Lost.

Like they have no idea what to do next.

***

An hour later, the paramedics and firefighters show up. By now we've swept up the glass and patched up the bloodiest parts of ourselves. The paramedics make sure Dad doesn't have a concussion. The firefighters test our fire extinguisher and find that it's working fine. Ditto with the fire alarm. Then they leave us alone with the curse.

The fire scorched the cabinets and pantry shelf but nothing else. Still, we don't go near the stove. We eat cold canned vegetables in silence. Mom and Dad still seem shell-shocked. I can't help thinking snarky thoughts. *Don't worry, guys, this wasn't just a bunch of random*

terrifying accidents. It was actually part of a curse.
Sweet deal, right? Just relax. We don't need the
negativity. We're living the dream.

I whisper to Morgan while we wash our
dishes, "We need to find that diary."

"We don't even know if it's here," she
whispers back.

"Only one way to find out."

*** *

By now it's late. Especially according to parent
time. On cue, Mom and Dad start yawning
and decide to go to bed. I can almost hear
their thoughts: *Maybe a good night's sleep will do*
the trick. Yeah, things will look better in the light
of morning.

I can't sleep. So I pull up the Internet on
my phone and type *"Emma Blake lighthouse"*
into the search bar. I don't expect any decent
hits. But I get plenty. This lady has her own
Wikipedia page.

. . . spent much of her childhood at Point
Encanto Lighthouse, where her father was the

lighthouse keeper . . . known for her daring rescue of four shipwrecked sailors in 1887 . . . rowed out alone in the storm to collect the survivors of the Laura Lee *. . . appointed keeper of the Martine Bay Lighthouse in 1895 . . . credited with saving more than twenty lives over her 52-year career . . .*

None of this is helpful as far as curse-breaking goes. But I can't help thinking *Man, this lady had balls.* One other thing I notice: she died in 1967, at the age of ninety-freaking-six. The same year that the skeleton tower replaced the original lighthouse.

* * *

It's still dark when something wakes me. I grab my phone to check the time. 2:17 a.m. At least it's past midnight. I don't remember when I dozed off, but the house is silent. So everyone else is either fine or dead. I'm hoping for Option 1.

I set my phone back on the bedside table—and freeze.

There's writing on the back of my hand,

letters traced in thin pen strokes. Writing I didn't put there. I'm sure of that, because it's in cursive. I only have vague memories of learning cursive in third or fourth grade. And I'm defining "learning" broadly.

For a solid minute, I hold my phone light over my hand, squinting at the cramped writing. Two words. I recognize a few letters—*l, t, o, n* . . . Slowly, my brain fills in the gaps.

skeleton tower

***

"Morgan. Morgan. Wake up!"

She punches me in the shoulder. My sister has a pretty strong right hook.

"Gah! Take it easy, Captain!"

"Oh. Jason." She sits up slowly. "Sorry. Reflex."

"I'm sure it would've worked wonders on the crew of the *Laura Lee*."

She ignores that. "We under attack again?"

"I don't think so. Listen. I think there's something else here besides the curse."

"Something *else*? Like one curse isn't enough to deal with?"

"I told you," I say. "There's being cursed, and there's being haunted. They're not the same thing. But maybe a place can be both at the same time."

"Uh, not following you."

"Look at this." I flip on the bedroom light and show her my hand. "It's different from the writing I saw on the mirror. And from the writing in the note. So who do you think wrote it? And why?"

"I have no earthly idea," she says.

"Well, I have a theory," I say. "Emma Blake. She's telling us how to find her diary."

CHAPTER 12

I feel less sure of myself once we're standing outside. But I try not to show it. Morgan shifts from foot to foot. Dad's keys jingle softly in her right hand. In her left hand she holds Mom's toolkit. She doesn't say anything. This is my idea. My show.

"Okay, Emma," I say out loud. "Where's that diary?"

I watch the skeleton tower's rotating beam. Am I imagining it, or is it slowing down?

Yeah, it's definitely slowing down. And then it stops. Its beacon of light stands still, shining directly into the top room of the old lighthouse.

One more glance at the skeleton tower. *Thanks, Emma*, I think.

***

This time the lighthouse door isn't already open. Morgan finds the right key and slides it into the lock.

Up in the lantern station, the beam from the skeleton tower is still lighting up the floor. Except for one spot.

Make that two spots. Two spots right next to each other, each the size and shape of a footprint.

"Uh . . . Emma?" I say. "Is that you?" I look at the floorboards where the dark outlines rest. "X marks the spot—is that it?"

As we move closer, the dark spots vanish. I kneel down and run my hand over the area where they were. The edge of a floorboard catches on my thumb.

"I think it's this one," I say to Morgan.

"Let's find out," she says.

We pry up the floorboard with flat-bladed screwdrivers. It comes free in Morgan's hand.

And in the hollow space beneath it . . .

One slim leather-bound book with weathered, yellow pages.

Now *this* is what I was picturing.

The beam on the skeleton tower slowly begins to revolve again.

***

Morgan is better at reading cursive than I am. She skims through the book, turning the pages carefully. "It's definitely Emma's diary. The early entries are from 1880, when she's nine."

"Can you skip ahead to 1887? Around October 25, the night of the shipwreck?"

She flips forward, almost to the end of the book. "Found it. The exact date." She starts reading out loud.

Father was blind-drunk again tonight. I fear many poor souls paid the price for it. A wicked storm whipped up around sunset. Shortly afterward, Father let the light go out. I was watching from the cottage, as always. I saw the beam flicker and die. I ran up to the lantern station

at once and got it going again. Father barely seemed
to notice.

Morgan trails off and keeps reading in silence.

"So what happened?" I press. "What else does she say?"

"She says she had seen the *Laura Lee* just offshore, close to the rocks. And it was gone by the time she got the light working again. So she knew it must've wrecked. She took a rowboat out in the storm and rescued four of the sailors. She's writing about this super casually, by the way. Just saved some dudes' lives, no big deal. Anyway . . . okay, this is interesting."

This will cost Father his position. He knows it, and he blames everyone but himself for it. He blames Mother for leaving. He blames me for tending his duties better than he does. He was actually angry with me tonight. Angry that I'd rescued these men. Because now these sailors will be able to report what happened. They are witnesses to his failure. So am I. So is the light itself. I fear he will never forgive any of us for that.

"Sounds like Papa Blake had some issues," I say.

"Yeah. I mean, nobody back then knew that alcoholism is a disease, so he probably couldn't get the help he—"

"Morgan? Can you find anything else in there about the *Laura Lee*?"

"Hold on, I'm looking." Flip, flip, flip. "Okay, so they find out her dad's getting fired . . ." Flip. "Dad's super mad. Emma feels it's only fair. The light deserves a reliable keeper. Sailors at sea deserve someone who can keep them safe . . . Huh."

"Huh, what?"

She reads another passage out loud.

Father says, "This light has brought me nothing but misery. It will bring only misery to its future keepers as well. It will test the others as it tested me. Show me a keeper who's willing to risk his own life to save another's." He glared at me. "Besides you,

*of course," he sneered. "Most people have the good
sense to stay out of trouble instead of stir it up."
I've heard him use that tone of voice before. Mother
called it his curse-casting voice.*

Morgan looks up at me. "I'm having a
thought here."

"Yeah," I say. "Me too. But see if there's
anything else."

Flip. "That was the last entry."

"Seriously?"

Flip. "Wait—there's one more. But the
writing's way different. Oh—I think it's just
smaller. Like—like she wrote this when she
was older."

*I've come back after all these years. I feel as if
Point Encanto still needs me. I know for certain
that it is still cursed.*

*People have always blamed the crew of the
Laura Lee. But I've never believed they were
behind the curse. Those four men I saved—they
forgave us. They understood. I like to believe
their less fortunate comrades did too.*

If anyone laid a curse on this place, it was Father.

The old light is being retired at last. They will replace it with a light that doesn't rely on human labor. Or fall prey to human frailty. This eases my mind. There will be no more keepers at Point Encanto. At least I hope not.

But if I'm wrong?

Just in case, I will leave this somewhere safe. The safest place I know.

My father's curse will always be here. But a piece of me will always be here too. Trying to protect you. Trying to help you. Whoever you are. Perhaps you will be the one who breaks the curse.

CHAPTER 13

"But she doesn't say how!" Morgan bursts out. "All this, and we still don't know how to break the curse!"

I can't argue with that. Or maybe I can.

"Remember what Emma's dad said when he was casting the curse?" I say. "Testing others? Risking lives?"

She turns back to the page. "Yeah. *Show me a keeper who's willing to risk his own life to save another's.*"

"So maybe that's how we break the curse. By risking our or saving someone else's life."

Morgan raises her eyebrows. "So we have to, what? Wait for someone to be in danger?

That sounds a little morbid."

"Maybe. At the very least, maybe we need to do our jobs well. Go above and beyond the call of duty. Or something."

She sighs. "Your earlier suggestion seems more practical."

"What earlier suggestion?"

"Leaving."

That catches me off guard. It feels wrong. Or at least, not satisfying to think about.

"I don't want to turn tail and run just because of some bitter dead dude," I say. "Not without giving it our best shot first."

I think Morgan's smiling at me. It's hard to tell in the dark.

***

I sleep late the next morning. Around 10:30, I stumble to the kitchen. Mom, Dad, and Morgan are already there, drinking instant coffee. They stop when I zombie-walk in.

"There you are," says Dad—not in his usual chipper way. Guess the night's sleep didn't work as well as he'd hoped. "Good. Time for a family conference."

Mom clears her throat. "First of all, we got a call earlier this morning. Mr. Shen had a minor heart attack on his way home last night."

Morgan gasps. I groan, "Oh, man. Is he going to be okay?" I feel bad about badgering him yesterday.

"He should make a full recovery," says Dad carefully. "But of course, this means no training for us today. And the foundation wants to shut down the lighthouse museum temporarily. Obviously whatever happened last night left a lot of damage. And we're not fully trained yet. So we're not qualified to run the site by ourselves."

"Not yet," I say. "But Mr. Shen can teach you the rest of the ropes when he's better. And will the foundation let us stay here in the meantime?"

"Yes," says Mom. "They'd like us to wait it out. But we're not sure if we should. All things considered."

I look at Morgan. Her face is grim. "What?" I ask.

Dad takes a long, sad gulp of coffee. So Mom answers me. "Dad and I have been thinking. Maybe this place isn't the best fit for us. Maybe we're not really cut out for this job. And we haven't put down roots yet. You kids aren't registered in the new school district. We haven't even finished unpacking. We could just . . . try something else."

Suddenly it hits me. They're giving up.

They've never actually done that before. Their plans have crashed and burned more times than I can count. But they've always had another plan ready. They've moved on, found new dreams. They've never just admitted defeat.

I remember what Emma said about her dad. How he'd disappointed her. How she'd given up on him. I think about how *alone* they both must have felt, living here. But they would've felt that way anywhere, probably. There's an entire atlas full of cursed places. The curses you bring with you, though? Those could probably work all over the world.

"Can't we at least give it a full week?" I

suggest. "Let's see how Mr. Shen's doing after a few more days. I know it's been tough. And, like, terrifying. But I think we can handle it. I believe in you guys."

I'm pretty sure I've never said those words before.

They're staring at me like I've sprouted an extra head. But they aren't saying no.

***

It's Morgan's idea to get our parents away from the lighthouse for the day. We need groceries, for one thing. And they need some time to, you guessed it, relax.

"Do something random and fun," says Morgan. "You'll pass through the state park on the way to and from town. Go on a hike or something." I can tell she's worried about them. It's hard to see them this deflated, this anxious. Maybe they'll feel more like themselves if they take some time to recharge.

They're onboard with it. Maybe because "random and fun" is their lifestyle in a nutshell. Maybe because they really do want to get away from this place.

They want us to come along, but we claim we'd rather stay behind and unpack. Eventually, they cave and head for the car. And we get to work.

We feel safer in the old lighthouse than in the keeper's cottage. So we set up camp in the lantern station. Morgan brings her laptop, and I bring a stack of books from the visitors' center. Our plan, basically, is this. Step one, learn everything about lighthouses. Step two, prepare for any possible disaster. Step three, be heroes.

We talk a little, but not about what we're really thinking. *Should we be rooting for something bad to happen?* Anyway, that's what *I'm* thinking. I don't want something bad to happen to random, innocent people. For that matter, I don't want something bad to happen to us.

A few hours later Morgan has a zillion tabs open on her browser. I didn't know that many articles on lighthouses *existed*. Meanwhile I'm halfway through *Lighthouses through*

Infographics. I hate it. But it's more informative than *Top Ten Lighthouses of the Western World.*

We're both taking notes in our school notebooks. Every so often Dad or Mom texts us.

Got groceries. Milk and eggs should be fine in the cooler for a while.

About 15 min. from home. Can see skeleton tower light from here. Stopping at a kayak rental place. How's that for random and fun!

That sounds more like the parents we know.

We haven't been paying attention to the time. Sunset creeps up on us.

The storm doesn't creep, though. It roars in like someone suddenly turned on a fog machine, a giant hose, and the mother of all fans. This is a window-rattling, foundation-shaking tempest. If there was any sun left in the sky a minute ago, it's gone now. The only light comes from the skeleton tower. And even that's sketchy in this downpour.

"I hope Mom and Dad finished kayaking already," says Morgan. "This is brutal."

My response is cut off by a crack of lightning, so close it sizzles. So close that it hits the skeleton tower.

The lightning bolt fades as fast as it appeared. Now it's dark. Completely dark.

The skeleton tower's light is out.

We leap to our feet. Morgan swears loudly. "That thing can't be broken! It's a legit navigation aid! Ships need that light!"

"Is it for sure broken?" I ask.

"I'll try to get a better look," says Morgan. "Stay here. Text Mom and Dad."

"Text them what?" I call after her. But she's already opening the door to the catwalk. She steps out onto the metal platform and goes to the railing.

I text our parents. *You guys OK? Be careful driving in this.*

The text doesn't go through. Because of the storm, maybe? Or . . .

I hear a rattling noise and look up. Morgan's trying to get back inside. Key word: trying.

The glass door isn't opening for her.

I run over and yank on it. But it doesn't budge. Morgan is trapped out on the platform. She's only been outside for a few seconds, but she's already soaked. The wind is tearing at her hair and sweatshirt. She looks scared. As scared as I've ever seen her.

"Jason!" she shouts at the top of her lungs. I barely hear her through the glass. "There needs to be a working light. You have to—" Something-something-garble.

"What?" I shout back.

She gestures frantically at something behind me.

I turn, half-expecting to see the ghost of Seth Blake. Instead I just see the giant lens.

Finally, I get it.

The skeleton tower—Emma Blake's gift— is dead. Point Encanto has gone dark. This part of the coastline needs a light.

It's time for steps two and three of our plan.

CHAPTER 14

"Mr. Shen, if I mess this up and ruin a historic light, I'm sorry."

I mumble this as I open the little hatch on the lens. Inside, the light bulb waits for me. I hope this thing has a surge protector. With all the lightning in the air, my life pretty much depends on no stray currents traveling through any wiring.

I manage to turn on the bulb without getting zapped. So far so good. Now I need to get the lens moving.

Slight problem: the lighthouse is starting to shake. I'm talking major shaking. Like an earthquake. Seth Blake's curse was not here to make friends. It was here to reduce this lighthouse to rubble.

I launch myself down the stairs. I'm going so fast, the spiraling of the staircase makes me dizzy. Then one of the steps falls right out from under me. Just comes loose and plunges all the way down to the floor. The clang when it lands is loud enough to carry over the sounds of the storm. Which is saying something.

I grip the railing hard and speed up. Another step falls away. And another. The whole staircase is collapsing beneath my feet like dominoes.

Three steps fall at the same time. Two of them were supporting my feet, and the third was my next-closest option. My body plummets. Luckily I already have a death-grip on the railing. My arms almost come out of their sockets, but I dangle instead of dropping straight down.

How far am I from the floor? Close enough to land safely if I let go of the railing?

The railing answers my question for me. It pulls away from the wall.

I crash through the opening in the staircase, left by the missing steps. I land on top of those three metal sheets. It isn't cozy. But I shoot to my feet again with no trouble. If I've broken any bones, they aren't important ones.

Now I'm standing in front of the clockworks. I grab the handle of the crank and start turning it. The massive metal weight hanging from the ceiling inches upward.

"Ninety turns," I mutter. I crank as fast as I can. The walls of the lighthouse shake. Outside, the wind sounds like a million wrestlers slamming into the building. I hope Morgan's okay out there.

I keep cranking.

The front door blows open. Instantly I get showered with rainwater. It almost hurts worse than the glass in the visitors' center last night. The floor is soaked. My feet slip. I almost go down but hold on to the crank.

My arms ache.

One of the fallen stair pieces flies up and hits me in the shoulder. Quickly followed by the rest of them. One narrowly misses my head. One gets me in the back of the knee. I do fall now. But I drag myself back upright. Still cranking.

"You know what, Seth?" I shout as I crank. "Not this time!"

The top of the counterweight touches the ceiling.

I take a deep breath. Since I can't get back up the stairs, I stumble outside. Through the pounding rain, I squint up. And see a beam of light streaming through the glass windows of the old lantern station. Turning with the rotating lens.

I also see Morgan, up on the catwalk. She leans over the railing and shouts something. I can't hear her, but then she waves and jumps up and down. The message must be good.

I whoop back at her. "We have liftoff!" Which isn't the right term to use, but whatever. I'm just getting started as a lighthouse keeper.

I'm so stoked that it takes me a few seconds to realize something else is changing. The storm.

It's dying down.

The wind fades. The rain eases up. It's still raining. And cold. And dark.

But not completely dark. Not anymore.

CHAPTER 15

Morgan has no trouble getting the catwalk door open when she tries again. If you're wondering how she gets down the ruined staircase, the answer is: *very carefully.* She also brings her laptop and our phones. The phones, by the way, are working again. Mom's calling me.

"We can see the light!" she gushes as soon as I answer. "We're a couple miles down the coast. We saw the skeleton tower go out . . ." She's so breathless I can barely understand her. "We were out in the kayaks. We went too far out and it was taking longer to get back than we expected. And then the storm! We couldn't see anything! We had no idea how close we were to the cliffs. But then the other light came on. Was that you two?"

"Um, yeah," I say. "The foundation will probably hate us for messing with the historic stuff. But it was kind of an emergency."

"It was amazing! I don't know how we would've gotten back to shore without it! We're on our way home now."

"Okay, Mom. See you soon." I hang up and look at Morgan. "The parental units are fully operational again."

She laughs. "And so is this lighthouse."

"Well—sort of." I gesture at the fragments of the staircase. "It'll need some fixing up."

"Yeah. Same with the skeleton tower. The coast guard will have to repair that."

I hope those repairs won't take long. Partly because I don't want to crank the counterweight ninety times every half hour just to keep the old lens rotating. And partly because that skeleton tower helped us. It's a piece of our ally, Emma Blake. I want to keep her around.

"So that was pretty heroic," says Morgan. "You turning the light on, I mean. Do you think it broke the curse?"

I look around the dark, damp lighthouse. All kinds of shadow footprints might be lurking here. Some friendly, some not. But that's true for lots of places. I think of the *Atlas of Cursed Places*, back in my room. Is the skull icon still hovering over Point Encanto?

I shrug. "Maybe. Hard to say. I guess we'll find out, Captain."

After all, Mom called Point Encanto *home*. And I'm okay with that.

ABOUT THE AUTHOR

Vanessa Acton is a writer and editor based in
Minneapolis, Minnesota. She enjoys stalking
dead people (also known as historical research),
drinking too much tea, and taking long walks
during her home state's annual three-week thaw.